Jacob's Eye Patch

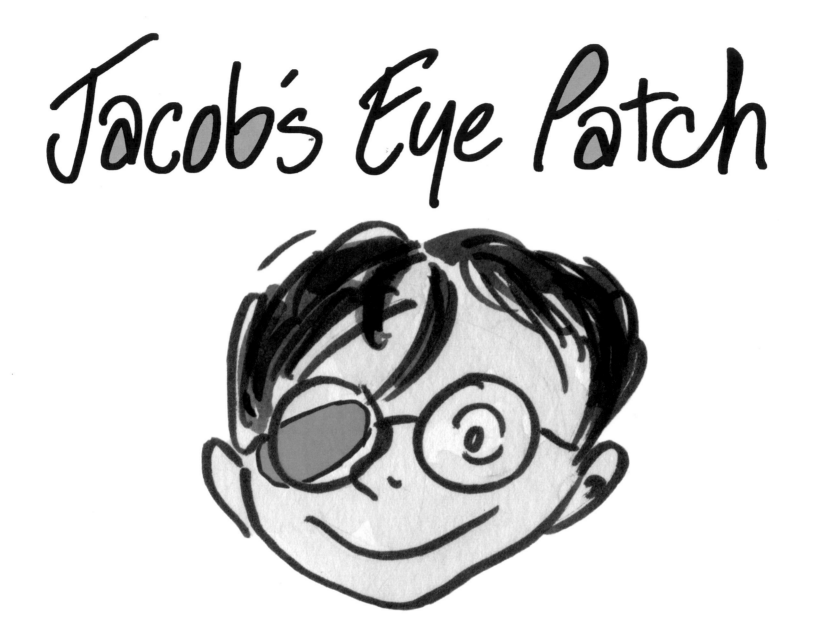

by Beth Kobliner Shaw & Jacob Shaw • illustrated by Jules Feiffer

SIMON & SCHUSTER

NEW YORK • LONDON • TORONTO • SYDNEY • NEW DELHI

Simon & Schuster
1230 Avenue of the Americas
New York, NY 10020

First Simon & Schuster hardcover edition September 2013

SIMON & SCHUSTER and colophon are registered trademarks of Simon & Schuster, Inc.

For information about special discounts for bulk purchases, please contact Simon & Schuster Special Sales at
1-866-506-1949 or business@simonandschuster.com.

The Simon & Schuster Speakers Bureau can bring authors to your live event. For more information or to book an event contact the
Simon & Schuster Speakers Bureau at 1-866-248-3049 or visit our website at www.simonspeakers.com.

Book design and layout by Katherine Roy

Manufactured in China

10 9 8 7 6 5 4 3 2 1

Library of Congress Cataloging-in-Publication Data
Kobliner, Beth.
Jacob's eye patch / by Beth Kobliner Shaw & Jacob Shaw ; illustrated by Jules Feiffer.
pages   cm
1. Eye—Fiction. 2. Amblyopia—Fiction. 3. Curiosity—Fiction.
4. People with disabilities—Fiction. I. Shaw, Jacob. II. Feiffer, Jules, illustrator. III. Title.
PZ7.K78785Jac 2013
[E]—dc23
2013016331
ISBN 978-1-4767-3732-4
ISBN 978-1-4767-3736-2 (ebook)

0713 SCP

Jacob and his mom were on their way to the science store to buy the most amazing thing ever—a light-up globe.

"Let's hurry, Mom, before the store closes," Jacob said. He had wanted the light-up globe for a very long time.

"Okay, sweetie, but first we need to pick up your brother from school," Jacob's mom said.
"Aw, Mom! I really want to get the globe!" Jacob said.

As they were walking, a woman stopped to look at Jacob.
"Excuse me," she said. "Why does your boy wear an eye patch?"

Now, Jacob knew his patch made people curious, and most of the time he didn't mind answering their questions. He talked about his patch—

at tae kwon do—

when he was walking
his dog, Milo—

and even once when
he milked a cow.

But this time, Jacob did not want to stop to answer the woman. "Sorry! We're rushing to catch a plane to Argentina!" he said. Jacob's mom *did* want to answer. "It all started when he was born…" She talked and talked all about the patch.

"Mom, please, we've got to go!" Jacob said. Jacob's mom smiled and said good-bye.

Jacob and his mom reached his brother's school. "Adam, I'm getting the light-up globe today! Let's go!" Jacob said.

Adam waved but kept talking to his friend. He talked and talked.

"Adam, we really need to hurry now!" Jacob said.

"Sorry to take so long," said Adam. "That kid asked me about your eye patch and I told him it gives you X-ray vision so you can see other people's evil secrets."

Jacob groaned and grabbed Adam's hand.

"Adam, we have to go!" Jacob said. "There's only one globe left at the store."

"Okay. But Jakey, it's Wednesday—ice cream day!" Adam said.

Jacob usually loved Ice Cream Wednesdays, but not today.

"Jakey, the ice cream store is right on the way," said his mom. "And Dad is meeting us for a cone. Don't worry, we'll get the globe."

At the ice cream shop there was a very long line.
"Look! Dad's at the counter!" Jacob said.

"Four cones, please," Jacob's dad said.

The server asked which flavors, and then he looked at Jacob and said, "Hey! I used to wear an eye patch. Why do you?"

Jacob did not want to talk about his patch now. "I don't speak English," he said.

Jacob's dad *did* want to talk about it. "The scientific explanation is interesting…" Then Jacob's dad talked and talked all about the patch.

Finally, they left the ice cream shop. "Rebecca just called," Jacob's mom said. "She's meeting us at the science store. It's just two blocks away."

They made it to the science store, and Jacob looked at the shelf and saw...

...that the light-up globe was gone!

Jacob was very sad and *very* angry about all the time they had wasted!

He ripped off his eye patch and threw it on the floor.

Then Jacob heard his sister Rebecca's voice. "Jakey! What took you so long?" Rebecca was holding the light-up globe!

"I had to fight off two screaming kids and a grandma to get this for you!" she said.

"Thank you, Rebecca!" Jacob said. He wrapped his arms around the globe. As his palm hit China, it lit up.

"The globe is so great," Jacob's mom said. She took a fresh patch out of her purse and put it over Jacob's eye. Jacob was so excited about the globe, he didn't notice.

Then, a little girl came over. "I love your globe," she said. "Hey, why do you have a Band-Aid on your eye?"

Now that Jacob had his light-up globe, he was happy to answer a question about his patch.

"It looks like a Band-Aid, but it's an eye patch," he said.

"When I was born, my left eye didn't see as well as my right eye," Jacob said.

"The doctor told my mom and dad to cover my right eye with a patch for three hours a day. That makes the left eye do all the seeing."

"Every day my left eye gets stronger," Jacob said.

"Cool. You look like a pirate!" the little girl said. "Can I touch Hawaii?"

"Sure," Jacob said. He saw that the girl had braces.

He was curious, but didn't ask her about them because she was having so much fun playing with the globe.

Jacob knew that he and the little girl—and almost everyone—have something that makes people curious. He also knew that sometimes you feel like talking about it, and sometimes you don't.

When Jacob is older, he won't need to wear a patch anymore because both of his eyes will be strong.

Until then, he is happy to answer questions about his patch anytime—

at tae kwon do— when he's walking his dog, Milo— and even when he's milking a cow.

Just don't ask him when he's in a big hurry!

Jacob's Note

I want to tell you what it's like to wear an eye patch. One thing is for sure: When I have a patch on, I always want to ask my mom or dad, "Can I take off my patch?" Some lucky times they say, "Okay, you're done with patching time." Other times, I have to wear it for one, two, or three hours more.

When you wear a patch, it blocks the light from your eye—it sort of feels like you're going to sleep only in one eye. The patch I wore for most of my life looks like a big Band-Aid, and the sticky side sticks to the skin around my eye. I needed this type of patch when I was younger so that I wouldn't pull it off all the time. When I was about six, I got a new type of patch that's like a pirate patch. Even though some pirate patches feel too puffy, I like them better because they are easier to take off when I'm done with patch time.

I felt embarrassed talking to people about my patch until one day in first grade. We were sharing stories about things we were born with that make us a little different, and I told my class about my patch. I was nervous about what kids would say at first, but afterward I realized it wasn't so bad since almost everyone has something. Now anytime anyone asks me about my patch, I just tell them.

A Mom's Note

"Don't stare. Don't point. And definitely don't say anything."

These are the rules we tell our kids to follow when they meet someone who is different—whether that person is in a wheelchair, extremely tall, or has brilliant orange hair.

For some reason, Jacob's eye patch prompts the opposite behavior. I like to think that it's because of Jacob's open, welcoming nature—one he was blessed with from birth—which acts as a kind of "green light" for questions about his patch. His ability to answer questions is empowering for Jacob.

Jacob wears a patch because he was born with two common eye conditions: amblyopia, which is when one eye (in his case, the right) is stronger than the other, and strabismus, more commonly known as being cross-eyed. When he was just five days old, the ophthalmologist told us to put an adhesive patch on Jacob's right eye for eight hours a day, forcing Jacob to rely on his weaker left eye. As he grew older, he had to wear the patch from three to as many as ten hours a day. Today, his eyes are beautifully aligned, with 20/20 vision in each.

Of course there are those times when Jacob, like any child, doesn't want to be bothered with questions. It can be irritating to offer up the same explanation day after day. But if someone really needs to know—more than Jacob needs not to talk about it—Jacob is always willing to tell his story one more time.

Authors' Acknowledgments

Only the genius Jules Feiffer could have tapped into the extraordinary gift Jacob gives to us all. We couldn't have had a better partner.

Thank you to Rebecca for being an amazing editor, Adam for his wry humor throughout the process, and Jenny and Sara for always getting in patch time. Big shout-outs to Danielle Claro for working her editorial magic on every aspect of this book; Leslie Schnur, who is as wise as she is funny; and Katherine Roy for her discerning eye. Deep gratitude to the absurdly talented Nick Greene, and to everyone else at Simon & Schuster. And the biggest thanks of all to Jon Karp, who always was, and continues to be, the smartest guy in the room.

To David, thank you for being the best husband and dad. As the expression goes, "The apple doesn't fall far from the tree," and we want to thank the orchard: gorgeous Grandma Shirley, delicious Grandpa Harold, and always cheerful Grandpa Irv. Memories of Grandma Marilyn's artistry inspired us throughout.

We are so grateful to Dr. Edward Buckley and Dr. Lisa Hall for their care of and dedication to our boy, as well as to Dr. Mark Steele, who is brilliant and kind. Thank you to the heroic Dr. Brian Campolattaro, who is as good a human being as he is a doctor. His ability and desire to use his extraordinary surgical skills for his patients in New York—and in the Dominican Republic and elsewhere through the Volunteer Health Program (www.volunteerhealthprogram.org)—is a beautiful thing.

This book is dedicated to a wonderful scientist and pediatric ophthalmologist, the late Dr. Arthur Rosenbaum of the Jules Stein Eye Institute at UCLA.